Catherine Rayner

VICTOR

The wolf with worries

MACMILLAN CHILDREN'S BOOKS

Wolves are

BRAVE and BIG and FIERCE.

They are very . . . wolfish!

Wolves do not worry
about anything.

This is Victor.

Victor thinks he is not wolfish enough,
and he is very worried about it.

In fact, Victor worries about pretty much everything.

Poor Victor.

Victor worries he is not BRAVE enough.
And so he tries pretending to be brave.

But then he worries that people might
believe him, and he might actually have
to do something brave, which is worrying.

Victor worries he is not BIG enough.
And so he tries pretending to be big.

But then he worries that people might think he is big enough to do things he is actually too worried to do.

Victor worries he is not FIERCE enough.

And so he tries pretending to be fierce.

But then he thinks that he might actually frighten the others, which is a worry!

Pretending doesn't seem to be working.

And Victor's worries start to grow.

Luckily, Victor has a best friend called Pablo.
"Hello, Victor," says Pablo.
"What's worrying you today?"

"I can't tell you," Victor whispers.
"Why not?" asks Pablo.
"Because if I tell you my worry," says Victor,
"it might become yours too, and worrying is
no fun at all."

"Hmmm," ponders Pablo. "But Victor,
I think it really is ok to talk about it.
If you share your worry, it will feel
smaller to you, but that doesn't
mean it will become mine."

So Victor explains that he is worried
he is not **BRAVE** enough.

And a funny thing happens.
As he talks, Victor begins to
feel a little bit better!

"Feel a bit better, Victor?"
asks Pablo.

Victor nods and he manages
a small smile!

Next, Victor shares his worry about not being BIG enough.

"Hmmm," thinks Pablo again. "Victor, I do understand your worry. How about you imagine putting it in a bubble and blowing it away? I can help you!"

So Victor and Pablo do just that,
and gently blow Victor's worry
bubble up into the sky.

"Feel a bit better, Victor?" asks Pablo
as they watch the bubble float away.

Victor nods and he manages
a medium-sized smile.

Feeling bolder, Victor shares his worry
about not being FIERCE enough.

"Hmmm," thinks Pablo once more. "I see.
I know what will help with this one.
Come with me!"

Pablo sets off as fast as he can.
Victor follows, and they run, and they
leap and they bounce through the forest.

"Feel a bit better?" asks Pablo as
they sit down to catch their breath.
"Sometimes it can help to take
your mind off things."

And Victor nods, with a large
smile on his face.

Because the funny thing is that while Victor was talking, and playing and blowing his worries away, he had started to feel rather ... wolfish.

"You'll never guess!" laughs Pablo, when Victor tells him. "I feel better too! I was worrying about all the same things."

"But Pablo! Other wolves don't worry!" says Victor, looking confused.

"EVERYBODY WORRIES!"
shouts Pablo.

And with that, Pablo and
Victor howl the biggest,
happiest, most
wolfish howl
EVER.

And do you know what ...

Victor still sometimes has his wolfish worries, because worries come and go. But that's ok.

Because he knows exactly what to do with them,
and that makes Victor feel

BRAVE and BIG

and FIERCE . . . inside!